WB:
To Katie, Martha, and Marian

JD:
To my nearest and dearest—
Mike and Graham, Mom and Dad

ISBN-13: 978-1-933212-26-5
ISBN-10: 1-933212-26-8

Library of Congress Cataloging-in-Publication Data

Bull, Webster, 1951-
A bad boy from Beacon Street : limericks / by Webster Bull ;
illustrations by Jacqueline Decker.
p. cm.
ISBN-10: 1-933212-26-8
ISBN-13: 978-1-933212-26-5
1. Boston (Mass.)--Juvenile poetry. 2. Children's poetry, American. 3. Limericks, Juvenile. I. Decker, Jacqueline. II. Title.
PS3602.U398B33 2006
811'.6--dc22

Printed in China

Visit Jacqueline Decker on the Web at www.jdecker.com.

Commonwealth Editions is an imprint of Memoirs Unlimited, Inc.
266 Cabot Street, Beverly, Massachusetts 01915
Visit us on the Web at www.commonwealtheditions.com.

A Bad Boy from Beacon Street

Limericks by Webster Bull

Illustrations by Jacqueline Decker

COMMONWEALTH EDITIONS
Beverly, Massachusetts

A young Red Sox rooter named Lance
Sat surrounded by much taller fans—
And the Yankees were winning—
Until the ninth inning—
When a homer fell right in his hands!

GO SOX!

ORTIZ
34

A grandpa from Southie named Austin
Was the oldest cab driver in Boston,
And still he maintained
That Boston remained
The easiest town to get lost in.

A proper Bostonian, Vance,
Took his wife, Mrs. Vance, to a dance,
But when they got there
How the ballroom did glare,
For the pair had forgotten their pants!

A marathon runner named Freddy
Lost by miles to a Kenyan, Ndeti.
Said Fred, still in pain,
"Maybe next year I'll train,
And maybe I'll eat less spaghetti."

A color-blind girl from BU
Took the Green Line to meet her friend Lou,
Meant to change to the Red,
Took the Orange Line instead,
And ended up feeling quite Blue.

Paul Revere saw two lights, got a horse,
And rode west on a zigzagging course.
All the way he did shout,
"The Redcoats are out!"
By the time he got home he was hoarse.

A bad boy from Beacon Street, Bart,
Puts baked beans in his mom's apple tart,
Then he listens with glee
While at afternoon tea
All his mother's fine lady friends fart.

On the Islands Pat liked to explore,
Sailed to Bumpkin, the Brewsters, and more,
Passed by Grape, Nut, and Moon,
Sheep, Calf, Deer, and Raccoon—
Didn't quit 'til he'd seen thirty-four.

A student could not understand
Why the Back Bay is nothing but land,
Why the North End is down
To the south of Charlestown,
Or the South End's above Mattapan.

Jamaica
Plain

Hyde Park

On the Frog Pond, Marie likes to skate,
Showing off for her friends Nate and Kate,
Hearing people say wow
At her double salchow,
And making her rear undulate.

Boston Bob likes to eat oyster stew,
Followed up by a lobster or two,
Plus steamers topped off by
A whole Boston cream pie.
No wonder his waist's 52!